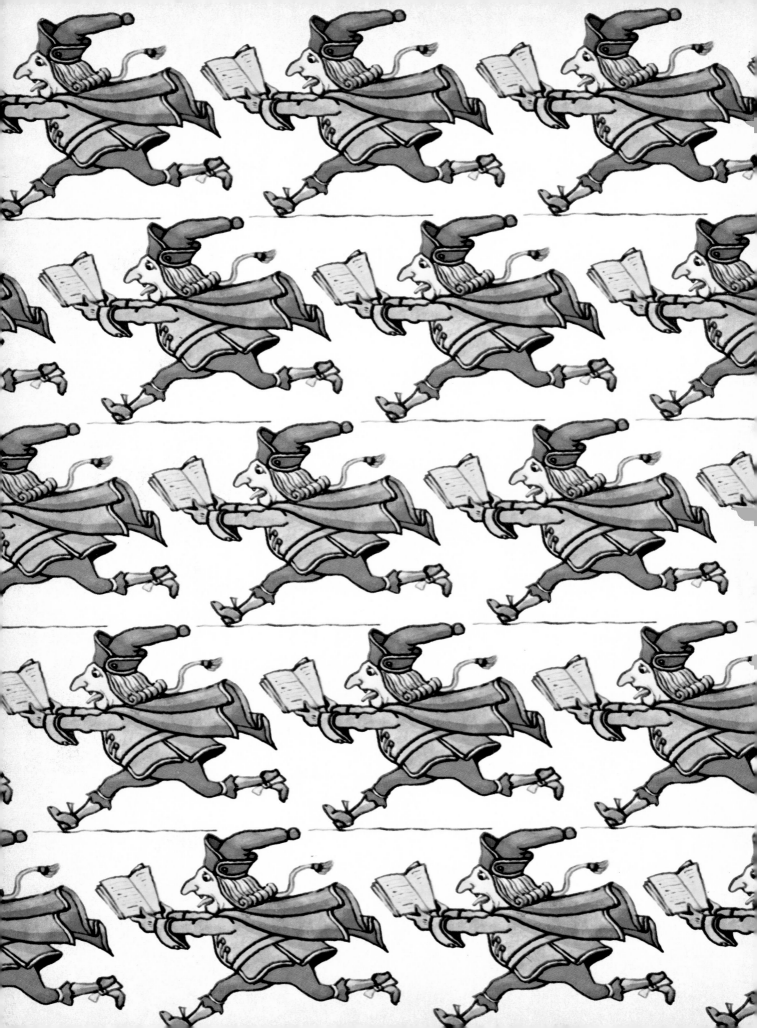

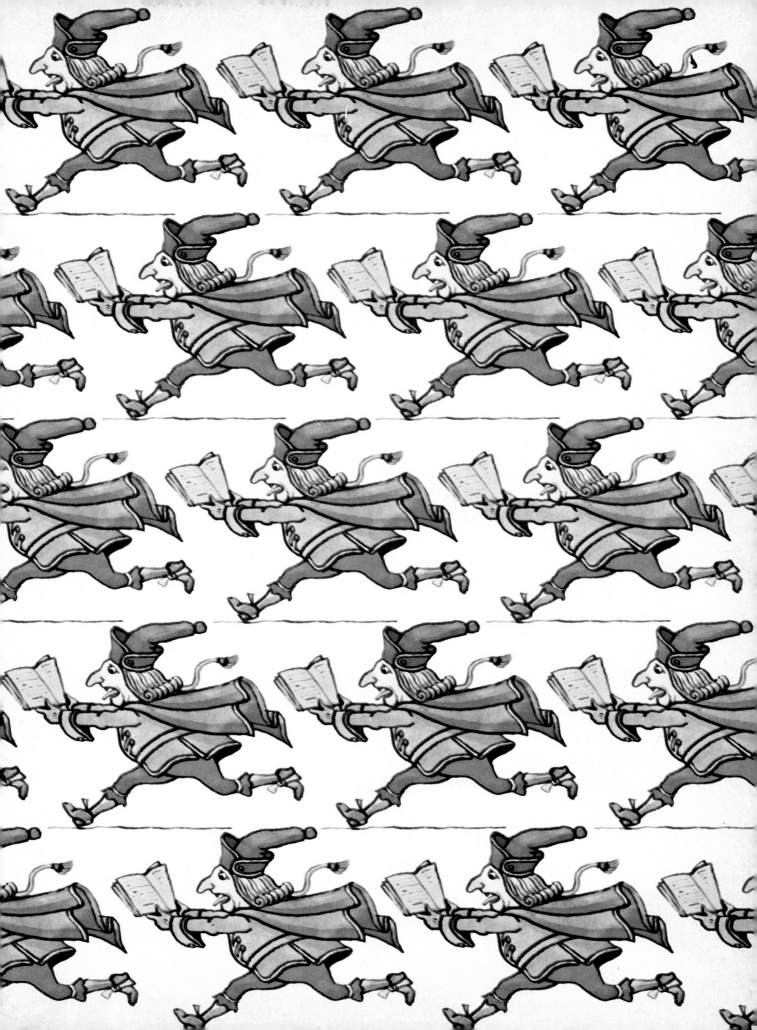

A STORYBOOK
FROM TOMI UNGERER

A STORYBOOK FROM TOMI UNGERER

Franklin Watts, Inc. • New York • 1974

Library of Congress Catalog Card
Number: 74-3504
ISBN: 0-531-02741-4
(library edition)
ISBN: 0-531-02742-2
(trade edition)

Printed in Italy

"The Wishing Table, the Gold Donkey,
and the Cudgel-in-the-sack," reprinted
by permission of Coward, McCann & Geoghegan,
Inc., from *More Tales From Grimm* by
Wanda Gag. Copyright 1947 by The Estate
of Wanda Gag.

"Petronella," text copyright © 1973 by
Jay Williams: Reprinted by permission
of Parents' Magazine Press.

"Little Red Riding Hood," copyright © 1974 by
Tomi Ungerer.

Alphabet illustrations copyright © 1974 by
Tomi Ungerer.

Contents

Changing Places

A Folk Tale
Adapted by Bernard Garfinkel

Once, not so long ago, on a farm in a green country across the sea, there lived a man and his wife and their little girl. On the farm, they had a cow and some pigs and goats and a gaggle of geese. Both the man and his wife worked very hard. On the farm, they grew barley and hay. The man plowed the earth and planted seeds, and cut the hay and barley. His wife fed the animals and cleaned the house and took care of the baby.

One day, the man came home after a long day of plowing in the fields. "Oh, it's hot out there," he said. "You are lucky to be in the house all day. You don't know how hard a man has to work under that broiling sun."

His wife did not take kindly to this remark. It happened that it was laundry day and she had done a great bundle of wash, in addition to all her regular chores.

"All right," she said. "If you think taking care of a house is so easy, we'll change places tomorrow. I'll go out into the fields and you can put the house in order."

The man laughed. "So be it," he said. "It will be a day off for me." He thought of how he would sit on a soft chair in the shade of the house, relaxing as he watched his daughter play.

The next morning, the wife went out into the fields, a scythe hanging from her shoulder, to cut the hay. Her husband smiled as he watched her go. "She'll see what it's like to do a real day's work," he said. Then, with his heart light at the thought of an easy day, he began to get the house in order.

First, he would churn the butter. That was easy work compared to plowing a row in the field. After he had churned for a time, he decided that he was thirsty. "A pint of ale would go fine now," he said to himself, and down he went to the cellar to get it. Just as he filled the glass, he heard scattering sounds above. It was the pig running around in the kitchen. He ran up the steps, quite forgetting that he had forgotten to shut the tap. He was afraid that the pig would overturn the churn. And when he got upstairs, he saw that this was just what had happened. The pig had its nose in a pool of cream and was grunting with pleasure as it lapped up the sweet stuff.

In a rage, he chased the pig out of the kitchen, catching it at the door with a kick that sent it sailing out into the yard.

He righted the churn, got a mop and cleaned up the spilled cream, then filled the churn with cream again. But as he put the cream pitcher down on the table, a thought flitted across his mind. "Oh, no!" he said. "It can't be." He wasn't sure, but he had a feeling that he might not have closed the tap on the ale barrel.

Down the stairs to the cellar he ran, hoping for the best. But it was the worst. A river of ale was spreading across the cellar floor, and the ale barrel was empty. "Oh, well," he said. "Accidents can happen." Back upstairs he went, ready to finish the churning. But then, suddenly, he remembered that the cow was still in the barn, not fed or given water yet, even though it was the middle of the morning.

So he ran to the barn and gave the cow some water, which she guzzled thirstily. Now he had to get her some food. There was plenty of grass in the meadow. "But that's too far to go," he thought. "I can't leave the baby alone."

The roof, he thought. That was a good idea. Like the other farmhouses around, the roof of his house was not tiled but covered with moss and sod, and a green crop of grass grew on it. In the back of the house, the roof came down close to a hill, and if he laid a plank across the open space, the cow could walk right across it and eat on the roof to her stomach's content.

So he did it, leading the slightly bewildered cow across the plank onto the roof. And when she saw that the roof was full of sweet grass, she began to eat hungrily. He came back around to the front of the house, feeling good at having solved this problem. But when he walked into the kitchen, he stopped short. "Oh, no!" he said. There was the baby, sitting on the churn. And before he could take another step, the churn tottered crazily and tipped over. Again the cream ran out, and the baby, covered with it, began to cry loudly.

He ran over, saw that the child wasn't hurt, picked her up and soothed her, wiping her face and hands with a cloth. There was no more cream, so they would have to go without butter at dinner. "Oh well," he said. "Accidents can happen."

hen he realized it was close to noon and his wife would soon be coming in from the fields for something to eat. He'd better work fast. So he set some sausages to frying, and then he put a kettle full of soup in the fire to heat. Just as he finished, he heard a great racket on the roof. "What is that silly cow doing up there?" he thought.

He raced outside and onto the roof. The cow had climbed up near the peak of the roof, where the angle was steep. Now she had her front feet over the peak and she was stuck. "That's all I need," he thought, "to have her fall off!"

Down to the barn he raced. He found a piece of rope and ran back up on the roof. He tied the rope around the cow's neck and, tugging and straining, pulled her off the peak. Then he let the other end of the rope fall down the chimney. Off the roof he raced and down to the kitchen. He tied the other end of the rope around his middle. "Now," he thought, "that silly cow will be safe."

He stirred the soup in the fire, turned the sausages in the pan, and began setting the table. "Finally, everything is under control," he thought, and he began to feel much better. "If only I had a glass of ale to quench my thirst, everything would be perfect."

He had just finished filling a pitcher with cold milk when he felt himself sliding across the stone floor of the kitchen toward the fireplace. "What the—" he started to say. But before he could get the words out, his feet lifted off the floor. Like the end of a snapped rubber band, he flew backside first right up the chimney, knocking everything—pots, dishes, and milk pitcher—off the table as he bumped against it.

ow he was stuck in the chimney, his head up in the blackness, his feet dangling over the kettle. The cow had slid down to the bottom of the roof, dragging him up the chimney as she went.

In a while, his wife came back from the fields. As soon as she was close to the house, she could see that all was not right. There was the cow, a rope around her neck, half on the roof, half on the plank leading to the roof. Her head was turned to her tail, and she looked as if she didn't know what to do next. There were all the pigs and geese running around in the vegetable garden where they shouldn't be. And there was the churn sitting in a puddle of cream.

Then she went into the house and saw that the kitchen was beginning to fill with smoke from the sausages burning on the fire. And there was the baby crawling about on the floor, a teapot over her head. "What is going on here?" she asked. "And where has that man gone?" She took the sausages off the fire. Then she picked up the baby, cleaned the mess off her face, and put her safely in a chair. Now she heard a muffled pounding coming out of the chimney. She looked in that direction and, for the first time, saw her husband's legs dangling. "God in heaven!" she cried, running over to the fireplace. "The evil spirits have attacked us."

"Cug me dowd," her husband shouted from up in the fireplace. His voice sounded ghostly but, thank the heavens, it was loud, so he must be all right. With the the scythe she began to saw at the rope. Her husband was shouting something but she couldn't make out what he was saying. And before she had cut through the last strand, the rope broke from his weight and down he slid, right into the kettle.

"What were you trying to say?" she said, smiling at the sight of him sitting in the kettle.

"I was trying to tell you to catch me so I wouldn't fall in the kettle," he said.

"Well," she said, "maybe you should stew in a pot for a while. It's probably what you deserve for saying that taking care of the house is such easy work."

"I'll never say it again," he said, "and I'll never want to change places with you."

And he never did.

The Tinder Box

Hans Christian Andersen

A soldier came marching along the highroad, left, right, left, right, a knapsack on his back and a sword hanging from his belt. He had been to the wars and now he was going home.

Around a curve in the road, he met an old witch—an ugly creature with a lower lip so long it hung down to her chin. "Good evening, soldier," she said. "That's a fine sword you have, and a large knapsack. You're a fine fellow, and I'm going to reward you. You shall have all the money you ever dreamed of."

"Thanks, old crone," the soldier said. "I'd like that."

"Do you see that big tree, there?" said the witch, her bony finger pointing at a giant tree near the road. "It's hollow inside, and if you climb to the top, you'll see a hole large enough for you to go down into the tree. I'll tie a rope around your waist so I can pull you up when you call me."

But what am I to do down in the tree?" the soldier asked.

"Why, get the money, of course," the witch answered. "When you get to the bottom of the tree, you'll be in a large room lit by more than a hundred lamps. Then you'll see three doors, and you can open them because the keys are in the locks. When you go into the first room, you'll see a large chest on the floor. A dog is sitting on it and his eyes are as large as saucers. But don't mind him! You'll have my blue apron. This you must spread on the floor. Then march up to the dog, lift him up and put him on the apron. After you do that, you can open the chest and take out as much money as you like.

"That chest has copper coins in it. If you want silver, go to the next room. There's another chest in there, and the dog on it has eyes as large as mill-wheels. Don't be afraid of him. Just put him on my apron and then you can take as much silver as you want. And if you would rather have gold than copper or silver, you can have that, as much as you can carry. Just go into the third room. The dog that's on the money chest in that room has eyes as large as a castle tower. A scary one, he is, believe me. But don't be afraid. Just put him on my apron and he won't hurt you. Then you'll be able to take as much gold as you want."

"That sounds fine to me," the soldier said. "But how much of the money will I have to give you, old woman? I guess you'll want most of it."

"Not a single coin will I have," the witch replied. "I only want one thing—an old tinder box which my grandmother left there by mistake the last time she was down in the tree."

"All right, then, tie the rope around my waist and I'll go down," the soldier said.

"Here it is," said the witch, "and here's my blue apron."

The soldier climbed the tree. He found the hole in the trunk and he let himself down until he was standing in a large room lit by a hundred lamps, just as the witch had said.

He opened the first door. Sure enough! There sat the dog with eyes as large as saucers, staring at him. "Nice fellow, nice fellow," said the soldier as he spread the blue apron on the floor. He lifted up the dog from the chest and put him on the apron. Then he filled his pockets with copper coins from the chest. He closed the lid, put the dog back on top of it and went into the second room.

Sure enough! There sat the dog with eyes as large as millwheels.

"Don't stare at me like that," the soldier said. "You'll make your eyes weak." Then he put the dog on the witch's apron. When he lifted the chest lid and saw all the silver coins inside, he quickly filled his pockets and knapsack with silver.

Then he went into the third room, and the dog he saw there was truly frightening. As the witch had said, his eyes were as large as the towers of a castle, and they turned round and round in his head like wheels.

"Good evening," said the soldier, and he lifted his cap respectfully, for he had never seen such a monster of a dog. He stood still, staring at the dog. "The quicker the better," he thought, and lifted the beast onto the apron. Then he raised the lid of the chest.

What a pile of gold he saw! Gold enough to buy the whole town—gold enough to buy all the cakes and sugar plums, all the tin soldiers, whips and rocking horses in the world. He quickly emptied his pockets of all the silver coins and filled them with gold instead. Not only his pockets and knapsack, but his boots and his cap he filled with gold so that he could hardly walk under the weight of it all. He put the dog back on the chest, closed the door of the room, and called up through the tree, "Pull me up, old witch."

"Have you got the tinder box?" the witch asked.

"My head's a sieve," the soldier said. "I forgot all about it," and he went back to get it.

The witch pulled him up and he stood on the road again, his pockets, boots, knapsack, and cap all filled with gold.

"Tell me now," he asked, "what are you going to do with this box?"

"That's not your concern," the witch said. "Just hand it over—this moment!"

"Nonsense," the soldier said. "Tell me what you're going to do with it or I'll draw my sword and cut off your head."

"No!" the witch screamed. "I won't tell you."

So the soldier drew his sword and cut off her head. He did not waste a minute looking at her. He tied all of the money in her apron, slung this bundle across his back, and with the tinder box in his pocket, started off for the nearest town.

It was, in fact, a fairly large city. The soldier walked into the best hotel, asked for the best room, and ordered an expensive dinner, for now he was a rich man. The servant who cleaned his boots thought they were incredibly old and worn for such a rich gentleman. The next day the soldier went out and bought new ones, and handsome clothes as well. With his gold the soldier had become a man to be reckoned with, and he called in the hotel staff to tell him all about the city, and about the king and his beautiful daughter, the princess.

"I'd certainly like to see her," the soldier said.

"You can't see her," was the reply. "She lives in a great copper palace, with walls and towers all around it. No one but the king can see her because it's been prophesied that she will marry a common soldier, and the king doesn't like that idea at all."

"If only I could see her just once," the soldier thought. But there was no way to do it.

The soldier led a merry life. He went to the theater, went for drives in the king's park, and gave money to all who asked, for he remembered how it was not to have a penny in his own pocket. He was always well dressed and had many friends who told him what a splendid fellow he was—a true gentleman—which he liked very much.

ut since he went about spending money freely every day and never got any back, he soon ran out. One day he found just two pence in his pocket. There was nothing to do but move out of his fine apartment into a tiny room under the attic. Now he had to clean his own boots and mend his own clothes. None of his old friends came to see him because they did not like to climb so many stairs.

One dark night, when he didn't have even enough money to buy a candle, he remembered that there was a small piece of candle in the tinder box he'd taken from the witch. He got the box out and struck fire with the flint to light the candle. But the instant the sparks flew out, the door to his room burst open and the dog with eyes as large as saucers stood before him and said, "Master, what commands do you have for your slave?"

"By heavens!" said the soldier. "This is a very nice tinder box if I can get whatever I want with it. Get me some money," he commanded the dog.

The creature vanished and in a twinkling reappeared with a large bag of pence in his mouth.

The soldier quickly realized what a treasure he had in the tinder box. If he struck the flint once, the dog that sat on the copper chest appeared; if he struck twice, the dog on the box of silver came; and if he struck three times, the dog that sat on the chest of gold waited for his command.

So the soldier, rich again, moved back to his fine rooms, and dressed in fine clothes and all his old friends came to see him again.

One evening he had a thought: "It's really silly that no one should be allowed to see the princess. Everyone says that she is so beautiful, but what's the good of it if she's shut up in that copper palace with all the towers guarding it. There must be a way for me to get to see her. Where is my tinder box?"

He struck the flint and in a flash the dog with eyes as large as saucers stood before him. "I know it's the middle of the night," said the soldier, "but I would like very much to see the princess—even if it's just for a moment."

The dog went out the door in an instant, and before the soldier even had time to think about it, he was back again, with the princess asleep on his back. He had never seen anyone so beautiful! She was so beautiful that anyone could see she was a real princess. The soldier could not help himself, he bent over and kissed her, for he was a true soldier.

Then the dog ran back to the palace with the princess. In the morning, when she was having breakfast with the king and queen, the princess told them about her wonderful dream that she had ridden on a dog's back and been kissed by a soldier.

"That's a fine thing," said the queen, not liking it one bit. And she instructed the lady-in-waiting to the princess to stay by her bed the next night, to see if it was really a dream or what it might be.

The soldier had a great desire to see the princess again that night, and he sent the dog for her. The dog picked her up and ran as fast as he could. But the old lady put on her galoshes and ran after him. When she saw the dog go into the soldier's house, she thought, "Now I know where it is," and she marked a large cross on the door with chalk. Then she went back to the palace. But when the dog was bringing the princess back, he saw the chalk mark on the door. He took another piece of chalk and marked a cross on every door of the town. That was very clever of him. Now the lady-in-waiting could not tell which door was the one she had chalked.

Early the next morning, the king, the queen, the lady-in-waiting, and all the court officials came to see where the princess had been the night before.

"Here it is," the king said when he saw the first door with a cross on it.

"No, my dear husband, it is there," said the queen, pointing to another door with a cross.

"There is one, and there is one," they all cried, and then they saw that all the doors had crosses on them.

But the queen was a very clever woman, who knew more about life than just how to ride in the royal carriage. She took her gold scissors, cut a piece of silk into small pieces, and made a pretty little bag. She filled the bag with flour and tied it to the princess's waist. Then she cut a tiny hole in the corner of the bag, just large enough to let the flour run out as the princess moved.

That night the dog came again, took the princess on his back, and ran off with her to the soldier, who now loved her very much and yearned to be a prince, so that she could be his wife. The dog never noticed the flour dripping out of the bag, marking a trail from the castle to the windows of the soldier's house, where he ran up the wall with the princess.

In the morning, the king and queen followed the flour trail to the soldier's house and the soldier was seized and thrown into a dungeon.

There he was, a prisoner, sitting in the dark of his cell, with no way to get out. And then, one day, the jailer said: "Tomorrow you will be hanged." That news did not cheer him up. If only he had his tinder box!

The next morning, through the bars of the cell's tiny window he could see a crowd of people gathering to watch him be hanged. He heard drums beating and soon he saw soldiers marching along. The whole town was coming, and among the crowd was a shoemaker's apprentice in his leather apron carrying a pair of shoes. He was in such a hurry that he dropped one of the shoes under the soldier's window as the soldier peeped out through the bars.

"Wait, wait, don't be in such a hurry, youngster," the soldier called. "Nothing will happen until I get there, anyway. But if you'll run over to my house and bring back my tinder box, I'll give you a penny. But you must hurry as fast as you can."

The boy was happy to earn a penny and he raced off, returning in a few minutes with the tinder box, which he gave to the soldier. And yes, now we shall hear what happened.

Outside the town, a gallows had been built, and soldiers were stationed around it. Behind them was the waiting crowd.

The king and queen were there, too, sitting on a beautiful throne, exactly opposite the judge and all the councillors.

The soldier climbed the ladder to the gallows. Just as they were ready to put the rope around his neck, he asked if he could be granted one last and harmless wish, such as a criminal is always allowed. He wanted only, he said, to smoke a pipe of tobacco, the last pipe he would ever smoke.

The king could not deny him this, so the soldier took out his tinder box. He struck fire with the flint, once, twice, three times and, sure enough, there were all the dogs standing before him. The one with eyes like saucers, the one with eyes like millwheels, the one with eyes as large as castle towers.

"Help me," the soldier cried. "Save me from being hanged." In a flash, the dogs rushed at the soldiers and the councillors. They grabbed one by the leg and another by the ear and tossed them so high in the air that when they fell back to the ground they were broken into pieces.

"I won't—" said the king. But before he could say another word, the largest dog, the one with eyes as large as castle towers, picked him up with the queen and threw them both up in the air after the others. The soldiers became frightened and the crowd shouted: "Good soldier, you shall be our king and marry the beautiful princess."

Then they led the soldier to the royal carriage. All three dogs danced in front of him, shouting, "Hurrah." Little boys put their fingers in their mouths and whistled and the soldiers presented arms in a salute to the new king. Then the princess came out of her copper palace to take her place as queen, which made her very happy. The wedding took place the next week and the three dogs had seats at the banquet table. There they sat, staring with their great eyes.

Clever Gretel

The Brothers Grimm
Adapted by Bernard Garfinkel

Once there was a cook named Gretel who worked for a rich master. Her master's home was large and fine, and Gretel was contented with her place and with herself. On her day off, when she dressed up to go out, she would put on her best red leather shoes and her brown velvet hat with one large feather. Then she would look at herself in the mirror and say, "Very nice. *Very* nice. You are a fine girl, Gretel."

Gretel was a good cook, and she loved to eat. She loved to drink a glass of wine or beer, too. Often she would have a glass when she was cooking. This made her hungry, and then she would taste whatever she was cooking. "A good cook has to know how her cooking tastes," she would say.

One day Gretel's master said to her, "Tonight we are having a guest to dinner. Roast two chickens for us."

"Of course, master," Gretel said. She caught two birds in the backyard, killed them, and plucked them. Towards evening, she put them in the fire to roast on a spit. Soon the chickens were crackling and turning brown. They were very nearly done, but the guest had not arrived. "If your guest does not come soon, I will have to take the chickens out of the fire," Gretel said. "They should be eaten soon, while they are nice and juicy."

"I'll run out and bring the guest back myself," her master said, and he dashed out of the house.

retel took the chickens out of the fire. Then she thought to herself, "I am so hot and thirsty from tending these birds, I'll just go down to the cellar and have a cooling glass." So she went down to the cellar and filled a tall glass with cold beer. She drank heartily and it was so good that she finished the glass and had another.

When she came upstairs again, she put the chickens back on the fire and watched them drip fat as they turned. Soon they smelled so good that she said to herself, "They look so good! But perhaps there is something wrong with them. I'd better have a taste and see." She dipped her finger into the gravy and licked it off. "Oh," she said, "it's a sin and a shame if these chickens aren't eaten right away."

She ran to the window to see if her master and the guest were coming, but she didn't see anyone. When she returned to the chickens she said, "Oh, one of the wings is burning. It had better be eaten right away." So she cut the wing off and gobbled it down. *Delicious.* Now she thought, "Well, if one wing is off, the master will see that something is wrong, so I'd better eat the other one as well."

After she had eaten the two wings, Gretel went to the window to see if the master and his guest were coming. They were nowhere to be seen and she thought, "Well, something has gone wrong. Probably they have stopped someplace along the way. So be it. Since the one chicken is cut into, it might as well be finished. First I'll have another drink and then I'll polish it off. Why should good things be allowed to spoil?" So she went down to the cellar and got another cold glass of beer. Then she came back upstairs and ate the rest of the chicken.

When she had finished the chicken, she looked again to see if her master was coming. There was no one in sight. "What is right for the one is right for the other," she thought. "The two go together." So she had another glass of beer and then she ate the second chicken.

Just as she was finished, she heard the master come in. "Quick, Gretel," he called. "Get the dinner ready. The guest will be here shortly."

Yes, master," Gretel said. "It will be ready right away."

The master went into the dining room to see if the table was set properly. Then he picked up the long carving knife and began to sharpen it. There was a polite knock, and Gretel went to the door.

The guest was an elderly gentleman. As he came inside, Gretel put her finger to her lips. "Be quiet," she said. "I'm afraid my master is up to no good. He invited you to dinner, but now he's talking about cutting off your ears. Listen, you can hear him sharpening his knife." The old man listened for a moment and heard the sound of steel against the sharpening stone. Without another word, he turned and ran out of the house.

Gretel ran inside to her master. "A fine guest you invited," she said.

"What's the matter?" her master asked.

"Everything," Gretel replied. "Just as I was carrying the tray of chickens into the dining room, he grabbed the two birds and ran off."

"That's a fine thing," the master said, his face turning red with anger. "Why, he might have left one for me to eat."

Knife in hand, the master ran to the door and saw the man running down the street. "Stop," he shouted, but the guest pretended not to hear. Out into the street the master ran, carving the air with his knife. "Just one, just one," he shouted as he ran after the guest—meaning that the man should leave one of the chickens.

But the guest went on running down the street like a frightened rabbit, determined to get home with both his ears on his head.

The Wishing Table

The Brothers Grimm
Adapted by Wanda Gag

Long ago there was a tailor who had worked hard in order to raise his three sons. Every day he sat cross-legged on his table and stitched away. But now, as he was getting old, he said to his oldest boy, "It is time you went out into the world to learn an honest trade so that you can support me in my old age. I haven't much to give you," he continued, "only a farthing and a pancake to start you on your way. The rest is up to you."

The boy went forth. On the first day he ate his pancake, on the second he spent his farthing for food, and on the third he said to himself, "Now you must find work, no matter what it is, otherwise you will starve."

Luckily, before the day was over, he found someone who needed help—a little gentleman who lived in a nutshell, but who was tremendously rich all the same.

"If you will not disobey me," said this tiny lord, "I will pay you well. All you need to do is to herd my cattle on the hill every day for a year. But heed my words! At the foot of the hill is a house from which issues the most lively dance music, but this house you must never enter."

And the boy said, "I will herd your cows well and will make it my business to stay away from the house of music."

He found it easy enough to keep the first part of his promise, but not so the second. Every day while he was herding cows on the hill, such sweet and lilting melodies floated up from the house below that the boy was almost beside himself with the desire to see what was going on there.

At last, one day long before his year was up, he was unable to control his curiosity any longer. "I'll just go a little nearer," he thought, "so as to hear the music better." But the nearer he went the gayer sounded the music, and before he knew it, he was in the forbidden house, dancing and singing with the merry folk who lived there.

When he came back that night the little lord came out of his nutshell and looked at him sternly. "You have disobeyed me," he said. "I hired you to work, not to dance and make merry; therefore I must send you away. But since you have done your work well in the time you were here, you shall not go forth empty-handed."

So saying, he handed the boy a little table. It was not much to look at, for it was plain and made of ordinary wood, but it had one remarkable quality. Whenever anyone set it down and said, "Table be decked," the good little table went into a sudden flurry, and in the next instant, there it was, spread with a snowy cloth and decked out with elegant dishes and silverware.

The boy thanked the tiny lord for this wonderful wishing table, and to himself he thought: "Now I will have enough for all my days. And my old father, he will be glad too, for with this handy table we'll never want for food, and the poor old man can at last give up his tedious work of tailoring."

So with a light heart he set out for home, and whenever or wherever he felt hungry, whether in field or forest or meadow, he took the table from his back, set it on the ground and said, "Table be decked," and there was his meal, ready to eat.

One night, when he was but a few miles from home, the boy stopped at an inn. It was filled with many jolly guests who greeted him cheerily and invited him to dine with them. But the boy said, "Oh no, I don't want to take those few morsels out of your mouths; instead, I would like to invite you as my guests."

The people, seeing that he looked far from rich, laughed heartily at what they thought was surely meant for a joke. But they stopped laughing and stared in astonishment when at his command, "Table, be decked," they saw the simple wooden table transformed into a festal board piled high with such delicacies as the innkeeper could never have provided, and from which a most savory smell rose to greet their nostrils. And what surprised them most of all was that as soon as any dish became empty, a full one would immediately appear in its place.

The innkeeper, meantime, stood in a corner and watched this in goggle-eyed wonder. "Such a cook would come right handy in your household," he said to himself; and after everyone else had gone to bed, he lay awake for hours wondering how he could get this wonderful table for himself. At last he remembered that in his rummage room he had an old table which looked just like the magic one. He rose and fetched it and then, creeping softly into the boy's bedroom, he quickly and quietly exchanged it for the wishing table.

Early the next morning the boy, suspecting nothing, picked up the table, hung it on his back and went on to his home. He was greeted with joy by his father.

"And have you brought anything back with you to help me in my old age?" asked the tailor.

"That I have," said his son. "See, here it is." And lifting the table from his back, he set it on the floor.

The old tailor looked at it from all sides, then said, "But this is just an old, poorly-made table!"

"So it may seem," said the boy, "but it is a wonderful wishing table all the same." And after telling his father about its remarkable powers, he added, "Now let us invite all our friends and relatives. They shall feast as they have never done before, for my table will set forth enough food for everybody."

When all the people were assembled for the promised feast, the boy set down his table in the middle of the room and cried, "Table, be decked!"

Dozens of eyes watched eagerly but nothing happened. The table did not bestir itself and remained as bare as any ordinary table which does not understand magic words. At this the guests, who were angry at having to go home as hungry as they had come, mocked him and called him a liar; while the poor boy, realizing now that he had been tricked by the innkeeper, hung his head in shame.

In the meantime, the tailor's second son had gone off to look for work. After eating his pancake and spending his farthing for food, he too found his way to the lord who lived in a nutshell. His experience was much like that of his brother. After herding the lord's cows for a while, he was lured from his work by the lively music which floated up to him, and tempted him to dance in the forbidden house. For this he was sent on his way by the lord, but not without a reward for his service.

His present was a donkey. "It is a peculiar kind of donkey," explained the tiny lord, "which neither draws a cart nor carries a sack. But he is useful all the same, for if you place him on a cloth and say, 'Bricklebrit,' the good animal will spew forth gold pieces for you, as many as you need."

"Well now, that is a fine thing!" cried the boy, and after thanking the lord for this remarkable gift, he set out for home.

After traveling two days he came to an inn, the same one—although he did not know it—at which his brother had been tricked out of his wishing table some time before. As he was leading his donkey into the barnyard, the innkeeper came to take it to the stable, but the boy said, "Oh, don't trouble yourself, I'll tie up the beast myself, for I must know where he stands."

"Hm!" thought the innkeeper. "I suppose he's so poor he must look after his own animal. Such a one will spend but little and is not worth my time." But when the boy handed him two gold pieces and asked to be given a good dinner, the astonished innkeeper opened his eyes wide.

After his meal, which was indeed a good one, the boy said carelessly, "How much more do I owe you?" and the innkeeper, eager to get all he could out of such an easy-going customer, neatly doubled the reckoning and said, "Two more gold pieces."

The boy felt in his pocket but found that his gold was at an end. "Wait a minute, Sir Host," he said, "I'll have to go and get some more money," and with that he whisked the tablecloth off the table and walked away with it. This made the innkeeper so curious that he stole out after his strange guest, but since the boy took care to bolt the stable door after himself, the man had to be content with peeping through a knothole in the door. When he saw the boy spreading the tablecloth under the donkey, his eyes fairly popped out of his head with wonder; and when he heard the boy say, 'Bricklebrit,' and saw a shower of gold pieces falling down on the cloth, he thought, "Well now, that's the easiest way of making money I've ever seen. Such a purse would not come amiss!"

This put an idea into his head, and that night when everyone was sleeping he went into the stable, led the gold donkey away, and tied up one of his own donkeys in its place. Early the next morning the boy untied the donkey and led it away, never guessing that it wasn't his own.

By midday he reached his home where he was greeted with open arms by his father.

"And what have you brought to help me in my old age?" asked the tailor.

"Oh, nothing but a donkey," said the boy.

"As to donkeys," said the old man, "there are enough of those around here already. A good goat would have pleased me better."

"Yes, but this is no ordinary donkey," said the son. "He is a magic one, and when one lays a cloth under him and says 'Bricklebrit' he spews out nothing but gold pieces. Just call together all our relatives and I'll make you all rich."

When the company was assembled for the promised treat, the boy brought the donkey into the room and placed him on a cloth which he spread out on the floor. Then he cried "Bricklebrit!" but no gold pieces fell, and this showed that the animal was nothing but an ordinary donkey who was ignorant of the art of making gold. The relatives, who were bitterly angry at having to go away as poor as they had come, mocked the poor boy, while he, realizing that the innkeeper had tricked him, pulled a long face and bore his disappointment as best he could. As for the old father, he had to betake himself to his needle again and toil for his living as before.

In the meantime the third boy had been sent forth with his pancake and his farthing, and with him things went much the same as it had with his brothers. He too chanced upon the little lord who lived in a nutshell, and was soon herding cows for him. The only difference between him and the others was that he, when going out upon the hill, stuffed his ears with cotton so that he might not hear the music floating up from the forbidden house. In this way he was able to serve out his full year, and for that the tiny lord gave him a present—a knapsack with a cudgel in it.

"Well," said the boy, "I can easily carry the sack on my back and it may be very useful to me, but why should the cudgel be in it? That only makes it heavy."

"I'll tell you why," said the lord. "If anyone does you any harm, just say, 'Cudgel-out-the-sack,' and it will leap out and pummel him so soundly that he won't be able to move for eight days, and it won't stop either, until you say, 'Cudgel-into-the-sack.'"

The boy thanked the little lord, hung the knapsack on his back and set out for home and, whenever anyone came too near him or tried to attack him, all he had to do was cry, "Cudgel-out-of-the-sack!" and instantly the cudgel would leap out of the sack and deal out a shower of blows.

fter two days of traveling the boy reached the inn where both his brothers had stayed, but since they had told him in a letter how the innkeeper had cheated them out of their wonderful magic gifts, he was on his guard against the rascal. Seating himself on a bench, he laid his knapsack on the table before him and began telling about all the wondrous things he had seen in the world.

"Yes, yes," he said, "it is not unusual to come across a wishing table or a gold donkey or suchlike marvels—all good things which I by no means despise—yet these are nothing compared to the remarkable treasure which I am carrying about with me in this sack!"

At this, as may be imagined, the innkeeper pricked up his ears. "Good heavens, what in the world could that be?" he thought. "No doubt the sack is filled with jewels; and in all justice they should be mine, for all good things go by threes." And from that moment his head held but one idea—that of getting the treasure for himself.

When bedtime came, the boy lay down on a bench, placing the sack beneath his head for a pillow. But the innkeeper did not go to bed. He waited until he thought the boy was sound asleep, then tiptoed up to him and began pulling very gently and carefully at the sack, hoping to get it out and to put another one in its place.

But the boy had been waiting for this for a long time. He was not asleep at all, and just as the innkeeper was about to give a final tug, the boy jumped up and cried, "Cudgel-out-of-the-sack!"

Well! Out came the cudgel, pounced upon the innkeeper, and thumped him on his back until the seams of his coat were ripped from top to bottom. In vain he cried for mercy. The louder he yelled the harder the cudgel beat out the time on his back, until at last the boy said, "Now then! You had better give back the wishing table and the gold donkey you stole from my brothers, or else we'll make you dance some more."

"Oh no!" cried the innkeeper humbly. "I'll gladly give back everything if only you'll make that confounded goblin get back into the sack."

So the boy cried, "Cudgel-into-the-sack," after which, leaving the innkeeper to brood over his misdeeds, he went to bed.

Early next morning, with the three wonderful treasures in his keeping, the boy went back to his home. When his father asked him what he had brought with him from his travels, he said, "A fine thing, father. See? A cudgel in a sack."

"A cudgel!" cried the tailor. "It was hardly worth your while going out into the world for that. You could easily have cut one for yourself out of any tree."

ut not one like this, dear father," said the boy. "If anyone wishes to harm me, all I have to do is to call my precious cudgel out of the sack and it will lead him a sorry dance, and it won't stop, either, until he prays for fair weather. And just think! In that way I have got back the wishing table and the gold donkey which the thievish innkeeper took from my brothers. Now let's send for them both, and for all our relations besides, and we'll get together enough food and gold for them all!"

The old tailor, remembering the experiences of his two other sons, was doubtful about the whole matter; nevertheless he called everyone together. Then the donkey was brought in, and the brother to whom he belonged set him on a cloth and cried, "Bricklebrit!" And, of course, since he was really the Gold Donkey, all went well and the gold pieces rained down upon the cloth like a cloudburst, nor was there an end to it until everyone had as much gold as he could carry. (I can see by your face that you would gladly have been there yourself!)

Next, the little table was brought into the room, and the brother to whom it belonged set it down on the floor and cried, "Table, be decked!" And, of course, since this was the real Wishing Table, it understood the magic words and did as it was told. Whish and whirr! there it was now, decked out with a clean white tablecloth, exquisite china and silverware, and loaded down with the most delectable food imaginable. Then such a grand and merry meal took place as the tailor had never known in all his born days, and the relatives stayed and enjoyed themselves far into the night.

All were happy and contented, but none more so than the old father, for now at last he was able to lock up his needle and thread, his yard-measure and tailor's goose, and to live in ease and comfort with his sons for the rest of his days.

Petronella

Jay Williams

In the kingdom of Skyclear Mountain, three princes were always born to the king and queen. The oldest prince was always called Michael, the middle prince was always called George and the youngest was always called Peter. When they were grown up, they always went to seek their fortunes. What happened to the oldest prince and the middle prince no one ever knew. But the youngest prince always rescued a princess, brought her home and and in time ruled over the kingdom. That was the way it had always been. And so far as anyone knew, that was the way it would always be. Until now..."Now" was the time of King Peter the Twenty-ninth and Queen Blossom. An oldest prince was born, and a middle prince. But the youngest prince turned out to be a girl.

"I'm sure it's not my fault," said the queen. "It must have been something I ate."

"Well," said the king gloomily, "we can't call her Peter. We'll have to call her Petronella. And what's to be done about it, I'm sure I don't know."

There was nothing to be done. The years passed, and the time came for the princes to go out and seek their fortunes. Michael and George said good-bye to the king and queen and mounted their horses. Then out came Petronella. She was dressed in traveling clothes, with a sword by her side and her bag packed.

"If you think," she said, "that I'm going to sit at home, you are mistaken. I'm going to seek my fortune, too."

"Impossible!" said the king.

"What will people say?" cried the queen.

ook here," said Prince Michael, "be reasonable, Pet. Stay home and wait. Sooner or later a prince will turn up."

Petronella smiled. She was a tall, handsome girl with flaming red hair, and when she smiled in that particular way it meant she was trying to keep her temper.

"I'm going with you," she said. "I'll find a prince if I have to rescue one from something myself. And that's that."

The grooms brought out her horse, and she said good-bye to her parents. Up she sprang to the saddle, and away she went behind her two brothers.

They traveled into the flat lands below Skyclear Mountain. After many days, they entered a great dark forest. They came to a place where the road divided into three, and there at the fork sat a little, wrinkled old man covered with dust and spider webs.

Prince Michael said, haughtily, "Where do these roads go, old man?"

"The road on the right goes to the city of Gratz," said the old man. "The road in the center goes to the castle of Blitz. The road on the left goes to the house of Albion the enchanter. And that's one."

"What do you mean by 'And that's one'?" asked Prince George.

"I mean," said the old man, "that I am forced to sit on this spot without stirring, and that I must answer one question from each person who passes by. And that's two."

Petronella's kind heart was touched. "Is there anything I can do to help you?" she asked.

The old man sprang to his feet. The dust fell from him in clouds.

"You have already done so," he said. "For that question is the one which releases me. I have sat here for sixty-two years waiting for someone to ask me that." He snapped his fingers with joy. "In return, I will tell you anything you wish to know."

"Where can I find a prince?" Petronella said promptly.

"There is one in the house of Albion the enchanter," the old man answered.

"Ah," said Petronella, "then that is where I am going."

n that case I will leave you," said her oldest brother, Michael. "For I am going to the castle of Blitz to see if I can find my fortune there."

"Good luck," said Prince George. "For I am going to the city of Gratz. I have a feeling my fortune is there."

They embraced her and rode away.

Petronella looked thoughtfully at the old man, who was combing spider webs and dust out of his beard. "May I ask you something else?" she said.

"Of course. Anything."

"Suppose I wanted to rescue that prince from the enchanter. How would I go about it? I haven't any experience in such things you see."

The old man chewed a piece of his beard. "I do not know everything," he said, after a moment. "I know that there are three magical secrets that, if you can get them from Albion, will help you."

"How can I get them?" asked Petronella.

"You must offer to work for him. He will set you three tasks, and if you do them you may ask for a reward. You must ask him for a comb for your hair, a mirror to look into and a ring for your finger."

"And then?"

"I do not know. I only know that when you rescue the prince, you can use these things to escape from the enchanter."

"It doesn't sound easy," Petronella sighed.

"Nothing we really want is easy," said the old man. "Look at me—I have wanted my freedom, and I've had to wait sixty-two years for it."

Petronella said good-bye to him. She mounted her horse and galloped along the third road.

It ended at a low, rambling house with a red roof. It was a comfortable-looking house, surrounded by gardens and stables and trees heavy with fruit. On the lawn, in an armchair, sat a handsome young man with his face turned to the sky and his eyes closed.

Petronella tied her horse to the gate and walked across the lawn.

"Is this the house of Albion the enchanter?" she said.

The young man blinked up at her in surprise.

"I think so," he said. "Yes, I'm sure it is."

"And who are you?"

The young man yawned and stretched. "I am Prince Ferdinand of Firebright," he replied. "Would you mind stepping aside? I'm trying to get a sunburn, and you're standing in the way."

Petronella snorted. "You don't sound like much of a prince."

"That's funny," said the young man, closing his eyes. "That's what my father always says."

At that moment, the door of the house opened and out came a man dressed all in black and silver. He was tall and thin and as sinister as a cloud full of thunder. His face was stern but full of wisdom. Petronella knew at once that he must be the enchanter.

e bowed to her, politely. "What can I do for you?"

"I wish to work for you," said Petronella, boldly.

Albion nodded. "I cannot refuse you," he said. "But I must warn you it will be dangerous. Tonight I will give you a task. If you do it, I will reward you. But if you fail, you must die."

Petronella glanced at the prince and sighed. "If I must, I must," she said. "Very well."

That evening, they all had dinner together in the enchanter's cozy kitchen. Then Albion took Petronella out to a stone building and unbolted its door. Inside were seven huge black dogs.

"You must watch my hounds all night," said he.

Petronella went inside, and Albion closed and locked the door.

At once, the hounds began to snarl and bark. They showed their teeth at her. But Petronella was a real princess. She plucked up her courage. Instead of backing away, she went toward the dogs. She began to speak to them in a quiet voice. The dogs stopped snarling and sniffed at her. She patted their heads.

"I see what it is," she said. "You are lonely here. I will keep you company."

And so all night long she sat on the floor and talked to the hounds and stroked them. They lay close to her, panting.

In the morning, Albion came to let her out. "Ah," said he, "I see that you are brave. If you had run from the dogs, they would have torn you to pieces. Now you may ask for what you want."

"I want a comb for my hair," said Petronella.

The enchanter gave her a comb carved from a piece of black wood.

Prince Ferdinand was sunning himself and working at a crossword puzzle. Petronella said, in a low voice, "I am doing this for you."

"That's nice," said the prince. "What's 'selfish' in nine letters?"

"You are," snapped Petronella. She went to the enchanter. "I will work for you once more," she said.

That night, Albion led her to a stable. Inside were seven huge white horses.

"Tonight," he said, "you must watch my steeds."

He went out and locked the door. At once, the horses began to rear and neigh. They pawed at her with their iron hooves.

But Petronella was a real princess. She looked closely at them and saw that their ribs stuck out. Their coats were rough and their manes and tails full of burrs.

"I see what it is," she said. "You are hungry and dirty."

She brought them as much hay as they could eat and began to brush them. All night long, she fed them and groomed them, and they stood quietly in their stalls.

In the morning, Albion let her out. "You are as kind as you are brave," said he. "If you had run from them, they would have trampled you under their hooves. What will you have as a reward?"

"I want a mirror to look into," answered Petronella. The enchanter gave her a mirror made of gray silver.

She looked across the lawn at Prince Ferdinand, who was doing sitting-up exercises. He was certainly very handsome. She said to the enchanter, "I will work for you once more."

That night, Albion led her to a loft above the stables. There, on perches, were seven great red hawks.

"Tonight," said he, "you must watch my falcons."

As soon as Petronella was locked in, the hawks began to beat their wings and scream at her.

etronella laughed. "That is not how birds sing," she said. "Listen."

She began to sing in a sweet voice. The hawks fell silent. All night long she sang to them, and they sat like feathered statues on their perches, listening.

In the morning, Albion said, "You are as talented as you are kind and brave. If you had run from them, they would have pecked and clawed you without mercy. What do you want now?"

"I want a ring for my finger," said Petronella.

The enchanter gave her a ring made from a single diamond.

All that day and all that night, Petronella slept, for she was very tired. But early the next morning she crept into Prince Ferdinand's room. He was sound asleep, wearing purple pajamas.

"Wake up," whispered Petronella. "I am going to rescue you."

Ferdinand awoke and stared sleepily at her. "What time is it?"

"Never mind that," said Petronella. "Come on!"

"But I'm still sleepy," Ferdinand objected. "And it's so pleasant here."

Petronella shook her head. "You're not much of a prince," she said, grimly. "But you're the best I can do. Come along."

She grabbed him by the wrist and dragged him out of bed. She hauled him down the stairs. His horse and hers were in another stable, and she saddled them quickly. She gave the prince a shove, and he mounted. She jumped on her own horse, seized the prince's reins, and away they went like the wind.

They had not gone far when they heard a tremendous thumping. Petronella looked back. A dark cloud rose behind them, and beneath it she saw the enchanter. He was running with great strides, faster than her horse could go.

"What shall we do?" she cried.

"Don't ask me," said Prince Ferdinand, grumpily. "I'm all shaken to bits by this fast riding."

Petronella desperately pulled out the comb. "The old man said that this would help me," she said. And because she didn't know what else to do with it, she threw it on the ground. At once, a forest rose up between her and the enchanter. The trees were so thick that no one could get between them.

Away went Petronella and the prince. But the enchanter turned himself into an ax and began to chop. Right and left he chopped, flashing, and the trees fell before him. Soon he was through the wood, and once again Petronella heard his footsteps thumping behind.

She reined in her horse. She took out the mirror and threw it on the ground. At once, a wide lake spread out behind her, gray and glittering.

Off they went again. But the enchanter sprang into the water, turning himself into a salmon as he did so. He swam across the lake and leaped out of the water onto the other bank.

Petronella heard him coming thump! thump! behind them again.

This time, she threw down the ring. It didn't turn into anything, but lay shining on the ground.

The enchanter came running up. He jumped over the ring. And as he jumped, the ring opened wide and then snapped up around him, holding his arms tight to his body in a magical grip from which he could not escape.

Well," said Prince Ferdinand, "that's the end of him."

Petronella looked at him in annoyance. Then she looked at the enchanter, held fast in the ring.

"Brother!" she said. "I can't just leave him here. He'll starve to death."

She got off her horse and went up to him. "If I release you," she said, "will you promise to let the prince go free?"

Albion stared at her in astonishment. "Let him go free?" he said. "What are you talking about? I'm glad to get rid of him."

It was Petronella's turn to look surprised. "I don't understand," she said. "Weren't you holding him prisoner?"

"Certainly not," said Albion. "He came to visit me for a weekend. At the end of it, he said, 'It's so pleasant here, do you mind if I stay on for another day or two?' I'm very polite, and I said, 'Of course.' He stayed on and on and on. I didn't like to be rude to a guest, and I couldn't just kick him out. I don't know what I'd have done if you hadn't dragged him away."

"But then—" said Petronella. "But then—why did you come running after him this way?"

"I wasn't chasing him," said the enchanter. "I was chasing you. You are just the girl I've been looking for. You are brave and kind and talented—and beautiful as well."

"Oh," said Petronella.

"I see," she said.

"Hm," said she. "How do I get this ring off you?"

"Give me a kiss."

She did so. The ring vanished from around Albion and re-appeared on Petronella's finger.

"I don't know what my parents will say when I come home with you instead of a prince," she said.

"Let's go and find out, shall we?" said the enchanter, cheer-fully.

He mounted one horse and Petronella the other. And off they trotted, side by side, leaving Ferdinand of Firebright to walk home as best he could.

Little Red Riding Hood

Reruminated by Tomi Ungerer

Once upon many times, in the middle of a godforsaken forest there stood a castle. In that castle lived a wolf. The woods were dark and pathless, the castle was sumptuous, and the wolf, like all wolves, was mean, broody, and ferociously ferocious. His reputation was even worse than his deeds. He lived there all alone—for he was feared by everyone—but for a rookery of ravens employed in his service. Wifeless, heirless, with whiskers turning to silver, he spent his days scanning the woods for some juicy fare.

One day, as he was gazing over a multitude of treetops from one of his many ramparts, there flew to him one of his watchcrows.

"Master venerable, lordly Duke and beloved ruler," he cawed, "in a thicket, three miles due northeast, beyond the moor, below the barrens, I sighted a little girl, morsel of a maiden, picking berries off your domain. She is dressed in reds all over like a stop sign.

Yes, master, as red as a little beet."

"Well done, trusted lackey," growled the wolf, smacking his flapping chops. "We shall settle the matter anon." Anon was right away and off went the wolf.

The little girl in red, her name was—yes, you guessed it—Little Red Riding Hood. Not the one you might already have read about. No. This Little Red Riding Hood was the real, no-nonsense one, and this story is one-hundred-to-a-nickel genuine.

She was as pretty as anything, pink and soft. Her braided blond hair shone like fresh bread, and birds could have flown off into the blue of her eyes. Besides, she had wit and sense. She was dressed in red because it was one of her mother's outlandish notions that her daughter might always easily be spotted that way. Little Red Riding Hood didn't mind. She thought it made her special.

Little Red Riding Hood was on her way to deliver a weekly supply of food to her mean and cranky grandmama, who lived in a run-down shack overlooking a greenish pond. The baskets she was carrying were heavy with three hogs' heads, two pints of rendered lard, two quarts of applejack, and two loaves of wrinkled bread. The old woman was a retired diva whose voice had gone sour. She was filled with superstitions and believed staunchly that she would restore her smithereened voice by eating pigs' heads—eyes, brains, and all. Her place was buzzing with flies who liked pigs' heads, too, in summer especially.

Little Red Riding Hood hated to go there. It was a hot and clammy day and her red Cheviot cape was itching and sticking to her back. The baskets were getting heavier and heavier, her arms longer and longer. Exhausted, she stopped in the cooling shade of the forest and started picking fragrant berries.

"I might just as well stop and be late and rest," she reflected. "These baskets are so heavy they feel as if something is growing inside them. All I get for my trouble is blows and insults, anyway. Each time I get there she accuses me of things I haven't done yet—that I guzzled off some of the applejack and nibbled at some pig's snout, and so on and so forth, and so beside the point, the comma, and the asterisk. I still carry on my tender skin the bluish marks of the old woman's beatings. And, here, look at the marks where she bit me in the shoulder last week. Vicious to the core, that's what she is."

"Hullo, there," growled a deep and raucous voice from behind a tree. It was the wolf, who had silently sneaked up on the trespassing child. "Hullo, cute damsel dear, what brings you browsing in my very own berry bushes?"

"Well, ho, you startled me. But yes, good day, Your Excellency," replied the damsel dear. "You find me here picking berries for my impatient little belly, and I was on my way to deliver these baskets here, full with food, to my mean and old grandmother who lives by the green fly pond, and besides I have noticed no trespassing signs ever, so how should I know whose bushes I am molesting, noble Prince?"

"Coriander and marjoram, lady young, lady bright. Maybe you are sassy, maybe you are clever, but I fancy your bearings. These baskets seem heavy indeed. Ha! Do you know what? I shall help you carry them. I am strong and efficient and it's a bleeding shame, if you ask me, to burden such a sweet little red maiden with loads like that. I know of your grandmother and all I can say is that her reputation is worse than mine."

"What is a reputation, noble Prince?" queried our heroine.

"Call me Duke," replied the wolf. "A reputation is what people think you are. Reputations come in all sizes. Some are good, some are bad or very bad, like mine. Anyway, here is my plan, and it comes from somebody who has far more experience of life than you. With my strong arms, I shall carry the baskets, not to your granny's bungalow, but to my very own castle. Come along, I live lonely and bored. Come with me and I shall share with you my secrets and more of my secrets. My vaults are plastered with treasures. You will sleep in satins and live in silks. My closets sag with brocade dresses on hangers of solid gold. Your winters will be wrapped in sable furs. My servants shall kiss the very ground you walk upon. I'll make you happy, you'll make me happy, as in a fairy tale."

There was a pensive silence and Little Red Riding Hood took three steps back in distrust.

"I was told wolves feed on little children. I don't quite trust you, Mister Duke. You wouldn't eat me, would you? With a big mouth like that, you could gobble me up in a jiffy and a spiffy, bones, cape, and all."

"Nonsense, child, mere slander, that is. Wolves feed only upon ugly children, and then only on special request," replied the beast with a sugar smile. "Never, ever would I do such a thing. Upon my mother's truffle, never."

"But your jowls are enormous, they look scary, and those huge fangs, why do they twinkle like that?" asked the girl unabashedly.

"Because I brush them every morning with powdered tripoli."

"And your tongue? Why is it so pink?"

"From chewing on rosebuds. Pink and red are my favorite colors," said the wolf.

"And why do—"

"Stop asking foolish questions," interrupted the wolf. "We must get started if we want to reach my palatial abode before dark. Besides, questions are bad for your happiness. Come along," said the wolf as he lifted the baskets. "Come along, there is an exotic library in my castle, and a splash of a swimming pool in my tropical greenhouse."

"But I cannot swim," said Little Red Riding Hood. "And what happens to my parents and my mean grandmother?"

"Read the end of this story, and you'll find out," said the wolf. "We shall send your parents post cards and invite them to the wedding. Your grandmother is old enough to take care of herself, and if you cannot swim all we have to do is empty the swimming pool."

Off they went to live happily ever after. They did get married and they had all sorts of children who all lived happily, too.

And the grandmother? Left without food, she shrank and shrank, until she was just inches high. When last seen, she was scavenging someone's larder in the company of a Norway rat. And, tiny and hungry, she was just as mean as ever.

That's ALL!

Tomi Ungerer has won world-wide acclaim as a writer and illustrator of books for children. His illustrations have also appeared in many magazines, and his paintings have been exhibited throughout the United States and Europe.

Born in Strasbourg, France, Mr. Ungerer came to the United States in 1956. He now lives in Nova Scotia and works on his farm.